Samuel French Acting

Breadcrumbs

by Jennifer Haley

SAMUELFRENCH.COM   SAMUELFRENCH.CO.UK

FOR PRODUCTION ENQUIRIES

UNITED STATES AND CANADA
Info@SamuelFrench.com
1-866-598-8449

UNITED KINGDOM AND EUROPE
Plays@SamuelFrench.co.uk
020-7255-4302

Each title is subject to availability from Samuel French, depending upon
country of performance. Please be aware that *BREADCRUMBS* may
not be licensed by Samuel French in your territory. Professional and
amateur producers should contact the nearest Samuel French office or
licensing partner to verify availability.

MUSIC USE NOTE

Licensees are solely responsible for obtaining formal written permission from copyright owners to use copyrighted music in the performance of this play and are strongly cautioned to do so. If no such permission is obtained by the licensee, then the licensee must use only original music that the licensee owns and controls. Licensees are solely responsible and liable for all music clearances and shall indemnify the copyright owners of the play(s) and their licensing agent, Samuel French, against any costs, expenses, losses and liabilities arising from the use of music by licensees. Please contact the appropriate music licensing authority in your territory for the rights to any incidental music.

IMPORTANT BILLING AND CREDIT REQUIREMENTS

If you have obtained performance rights to this title, please refer to your licensing agreement for important billing and credit requirements.

BREADCRUMBS was first produced by the Contemporary American Theater Festival at Studio Theater in Shepherdstown, West Virginia on July 10, 2010. The performance was directed by Laura Kepley, with sets by Robert Klingelhoefer, costumes by Ivania Stack, lights by Colin Bills, and sound and composition by Matt Nielson. The Production Stage Manager was Lori M. Doyle. The cast was as follows:

ALIDA . . . . Helen-Jean Arthur
BETH/MOTHER . . . . Eva Kaminsky

CHARACTERS

ALIDA – a reclusive writer, somewhere in her sixties, diagnosed with Alzheimer's

BETH/MOTHER – a chaotic drifter, somewhere around thirty, looking for a home

SETTING

Alida's apartment, various locales around the country, and the deep, dark woods.

For my mother

WOODS

*(**ALIDA** writes on sticky notes. One word per note. She drops them as she walks along the path.)*

ALIDA. Words. Window sills. Yellow leaves. High heels. Etymology. Sticky notes. Text Messages. Stuffed Animals. Basements. Fortune cookies. Bones.

(She glances around. Spooked. She continues.)

Peep shows. Fairy tales. Boyfriends. Dark woods. Twisting paths. Breadcrumbs. They point the way back. To something familiar.

(She glances backward. The sticky notes are gone. Gasp!)

Until they are stolen, by the squirrels. And the only way out, is the only way in. The only way forward. Is to the light. Of the witch's house.

*(In the clearing, a house becomes visible. The witch stands inside the doorway, silhouetted against the light. She moves to a table in the woods. Nods to the seat across from her. **ALIDA** reluctantly sits. The witch pulls off her mask. Underneath is **BETH**.)*

DIAGNOSIS

(A clinic. Cold. **BETH** *wears a lab coat.)*

BETH. Do you find you misplace things?

ALIDA. Yes. I. Yes.

BETH. When you go out, do you forget how to get home?

ALIDA. I don't go out any more.

BETH. Does your family notice a difference in you?

ALIDA. I live alone.

BETH. Okay Fran. Can I call you Fran?

ALIDA. My name is Alida.

BETH. Alida. You're not Fran?

ALIDA. No I'm not Fran.

BETH. Wait. Oh. I got the wrong chart. Hold on. Here we go. Today's nuts. I'm losing my mind.

> *(***ALIDA*** *stares at her.* ***BETH*** *realizes her gaffe.)*

Sorry. Uh. Sorry. SO! Alida. Can I call you Alida?

ALIDA. You *may.*

BETH. I'm Beth. It says right here on my name tag. Beth.

ALIDA. Beth.

BETH. And it says here you're a writer.

ALIDA. I am. A writer.

BETH. That's so cool! What kind of stuff do you write?

ALIDA. Stuff?

BETH. I mean like books? Poetry?

ALIDA. Is this part of the exam?

BETH. No. I was just. Getting to know you.

> *(***ALIDA*** *stares at her.* ***BETH***, *nervous, consults a brochure.)*

Okay Alida. I'm going to administer a diagnostic test. First I will recite ten different words to you. Try to remember these because I'm going to ask you about them later. Ready? Squirrel. Squirrel. Squirrel.

Squirrel. Squirrel. Squirrel. Squirrel. Squirrel. Squirrel. Squirrel. Got it?

(**ALIDA** *absorbs the words as though each one is different.*)

ALIDA. Got it.

BETH. Next I'm going to tell you a word, and I want you to spell it for me. The word is: optimistic.

ALIDA. Optimistic?

BETH. Optimistic.

ALIDA. *(annoyed)* Right. O. P. T. I. M. I. S. T. I. C.

BETH. Now I want you to spell it backwards.

ALIDA. C. I. T. I. *(She stops.)*

BETH. Keep going.

ALIDA. S. M. T. O.

BETH. Great! Now I'm going to recite a story to you, and when I'm done, you will recite it back to me. Got it? Once upon a time…

(Something changes.)

There was a little girl whose parents gave her so many stuffed animals she didn't know how to love them all. There was Bunny and Bear B and and Durndell and Gerger Meal and Mustafus Otter Brown and Wormy and Scrotal and Flopsalot and…well it went on, she had so many stuffed animals she couldn't sleep with all of them, so she developed a system where she called her bed the Home, and a box next to her bed the Hotel, and every night she would rotate sets of animals from the Hotel to the Home so she could fill each one with fair and regular love. When the girl grew up, she put them in a big, black garbage bag and hauled them from one boyfriend to the next, long after her parents told her they didn't want her to be their daughter any more.

(Something changes back.)

Okay Alida, would you please recite that story back to me as you remember it?

ALIDA. Let's see. Once upon a time…

(Something changes.)

There was a little girl whose mother dragged her from one end of the forest to the next in search of Prince Charming. They traveled through briars and bogs, through mountains and valleys, through snow and ice and wind. Every night, bundled together against the cold, the mother would whisper to the girl, Tomorrow, tomorrow, tomorrow we will find him. And then one day, the little girl awoke to find her mother – gone. All the Princes, it seemed, were looking for women who were unencumbered. So the girl became a writer, because filling the world's emptiness with words was the only way to go on living in it –

(Something changes back. **BETH** *looks at* **ALIDA** *strangely.)*

That's not the story, is it? I'm not doing it correctly.

BETH. There is no correct way. You do the best you can.

ALIDA. But I'm not – I can't remember it the way you told it.

BETH. *(too chipper)* That's fine! There's no right and wrong here. It's simply diagnostic. Now, I want you to think back to that list of ten different words I recited before the story. Can you tell me what some of them were?

ALIDA. Squirrel.

BETH. And.

ALIDA. Squirrel.

BETH. That's one of them. Can you remember the others?

*(***ALIDA*** realizes she cannot.)*

ALIDA. Um…squirrel?

BETH. Okay, Alida, I'm going to give your test results to the doctor, and he will contact you to go over his findings. You should expect a phone call in about a week –

ALIDA. What are the findings?

BETH. I'm sorry, but only the doctor can interpret them.

ALIDA. I want to know now.

BETH. I'm just a nurse's aide. I'm not supposed to talk to patients about their diagnosis.

ALIDA. Don't fuck with me. It's –

(She can't say the word. Pause. **BETH** *nods.)*

And there's no cure.

*(***BETH*** *shakes her head.)*

Why even bother diagnosing it?

BETH. It's so families can start making. Arrangements.

ALIDA. What about women? Who live alone?

WINDOWSILLS

*(**ALIDA**'s apartment. Small and spare. **BETH** stands in the doorway, an enormous handbag over her shoulder, clutching a manila folder. **ALIDA** faces her in combat stance.)*

ALIDA. Who let you in?

BETH. The door was open.

ALIDA. I don't leave my door open.

BETH. I came up the stairs, and the door was –

ALIDA. Who let you up?

BETH. You buzzed me.

ALIDA. I did not.

BETH. Someone buzzed me. I pushed the bell, and there was a buzz.

ALIDA. It wasn't me.

BETH. I'm sorry.

ALIDA. Get out.

BETH. Okay. It's just. You left this at the clinic.

(She proffers the manila folder.)

ALIDA. I've been looking for that.

BETH. It was on the counter. By the Q-tips.

ALIDA. I don't remember taking it with me.

BETH. Is it a new story?

ALIDA. Did you read it?

BETH. No, no. Of course not. We respect our patients' privacy.

ALIDA. Uh huh.

*(**ALIDA** reaches for the folder. **BETH** hands it to her. Hovers.)*

BETH. I read one of your other stories. All last night. I found it at the bookstore. I couldn't believe it. I went to the bookstore, looked up your name, and there they were. All your books. That must be amazing. To see your name on all these stories that other people read. "Fractured fairy tales for the literati." That's what it said on the inside cover. I don't know if I count as literati. I got my degree at the community college. But I loved the story about the girl stuck in the dungeon of a high rise castle. It reminded me of a temp job where I worked on catastrophic claims for a workers compensation insurance company, and I had to have a security badge to get into this windowless basement room, and all day long I went through files of people who like got their hands chopped off in machinery or were shot by disgruntled co-workers –

ALIDA. How did you find me?

BETH. Your address was on your chart.

ALIDA. So was my phone number.

BETH. You're on my way home.

ALIDA. Does the clinic know you're here?

BETH. Sure.

ALIDA. Perhaps I should let them know you came by.

BETH. No! Please. I mean. I thought I'd –

ALIDA. Before I call them, I think you should –

BETH. Go. Right. Okay. Thank you.

(**BETH** *leaves, instantly returns.*)

I almost forgot! These were downstairs by the mailbox.

(**BETH** *produces a bundle of envelopes from her giant bag, hands it to* **ALIDA.**)

Fans?

ALIDA. I don't have fans.

BETH. They look like they're from people –

ALIDA. Football players have fans. Rockstars have fans. I have individuals who appreciate my work.

BETH. Isn't that –

ALIDA. And they are irrelevant to me because I write only for myself.

(**ALIDA** *chunks the envelopes in the trash.*)

BETH. You don't have to do that. Just because –

ALIDA. Because what?

BETH. Because of your diagnosis.

ALIDA. I did not receive a diagnosis.

BETH. At the clinic.

ALIDA. You said only a doctor could give me a diagnosis. I did not speak to a doctor.

BETH. But the story you told to me. It was different.

ALIDA. I told the same story differently.

BETH. Do you want to tell *this* story?

(*She gestures to the manila folder, tucked under* **ALIDA**'s *arm.* **ALIDA** *stares down at it. Beat.*)

ALIDA. The other morning. There was a leaf on the windowsill. A yellow leaf. And I realized. It's Fall. It's Fall again. The leaf looked like my hand. With all its veins. Reaching out. And I thought, maybe I should write my memories. Before my brain. Turns brown.

BETH. If you want any help. I don't know anything about writing. But I'm good at taking notes.

(**ALIDA** *snaps out of it.*)

ALIDA. I don't need any help.

BETH. I'm only part time at the clinic.

ALIDA. I don't like people in my apartment.

BETH. And I am – an individual who appreciates your work.

ALIDA. Especially sycophants. Get out. I have everything under…everything under…

BETH. Control?

BOYFRIENDS

(BETH *sits at* ALIDA*'s table with her day planner.* ALIDA *stands over her.*)

ALIDA. I will expect you here from six a.m. to ten a.m.

BETH. Six a.m.?

ALIDA. My best time to work is in the morning.

BETH. I'm due at the clinic by nine. Except for Wednesday. How about that morning we split the difference with…eight a.m. to noon? And maybe Tuesdays and Thursdays we could do two p.m. to six. Except, duh, I have therapy on Thursday afternoons. Maybe we could do an evening session – I could bring takeout –

ALIDA. This is not a negotiable system.

BETH. Oh.

ALIDA. And probably not a good idea.

BETH. Wait. Let me talk to one of the doctors about moving my shift around.

ALIDA. I have notepads here. Please bring your own pens. Make sure they are working.

BETH. I have a laptop. I'll bring that.

ALIDA. A what?

BETH. A laptop computer.

ALIDA. Oh no no no. I only work longhand.

BETH. But I type faster than I write.

ALIDA. This is about quality, not quantity. This is about ink on paper, not zeroes and ones. This is about none of the material leaving my apartment.

BETH. I would never –

ALIDA. No? I don't know you. I don't know you at all. In fact, I don't think –

BETH. I'll bring pens! Lots of pens. Working pens…

(*She makes a note in her day planner. Smiles brightly at* ALIDA.)

ALIDA. You'll be sent to the library on occasion. I assume
    you have a card.

BETH. I tried to get one. They want a local address.

ALIDA. You don't have a local address?

BETH. I live with my boyfriend.

ALIDA. Don't you pay bills?

BETH. It's his apartment. I moved in three months ago.

ALIDA. What about your previous residence?

BETH. That was. Another boyfriend.

ALIDA. Another boyfriend?

BETH. *(shrugs)* I like guys.

ALIDA. I know the type. Listen…what's your name again?

BETH. *(points to her name tag)* Beth.

ALIDA. Listen, Beth, what do you think qualifies you for
    this position?

BETH. This is a position? I thought I was helping out.

ALIDA. I told you I do not want "help." I'll be paying you
    every two weeks.

BETH. Really?

ALIDA. You were going to do this for free?

BETH. I thought. I might learn something.

ALIDA. This is not an apprenticeship. I am not a teacher.

BETH. But I'm sure the experience –

ALIDA. Will mainly involve research. And keeping my
    thoughts together.

BETH. Such thoughts. I had this job once as a cocktail
    waitress, and my regulars had so many stories. I fell
    in love with them. Not like, love love, but secret love,
    because they were so sad. I brought them stiff drinks
    and a big smile, and for a little while I made them
    happy, listening to their sad stories. I tried to write
    them down. I couldn't put them together in a way that
    made them live. So when I read that paragraph. About
    your mother brushing your hair. And I saw her so
    clearly, in just a few words. I thought, if I could learn
    to tell a story –

ALIDA. How do you know about the mother?

BETH. You left your story at the clinic.

ALIDA. You said you didn't read it.

BETH. I glanced inside to see what it was. I scanned the first page.

ALIDA. The mother doesn't appear on the first page.

BETH. Oh. Well. Perhaps I read a few more.

ALIDA. So you were lying to me?

BETH. No. I just loved it and – *(pause).* Why do you call her "the" mother when it's your mother?

ALIDA. This is a work of fiction.

BETH. It sounds like an autobiography.

ALIDA. How much did you read?

BETH. If I'm helping you, I'm going to have to read –

ALIDA. You are not helping –

BETH. Working for you – if I'm working for you –

ALIDA. You are *not* working for me. And you *will not be* working for me. You are clearly someone I cannot trust.

(BETH slowly closes her day planner.)

BETH. Long term memories remain intact, but the patient finds it harder to relay them as the short term memories come and go.

ALIDA. That sounds like a threat.

BETH. I've been working at the clinic a year now. I know this disease. You'll have to trust someone if you want to finish your story.

(BETH reaches in her bag and pulls out a hair brush. Something changes.)

BREADCRUMBS

(**BETH** *becomes* **MOTHER**. **ALIDA** *becomes herself as a child*. **MOTHER** *brushes* **ALIDA**'s *hair. They stare forward into a mirror*.)

ALIDA. Once upon a time there was a girl named Gretel, who lived with her mother at the edge of a deep, dark woods. One day Prince Charming came to call, so the mother sent Gretel to the woods to gather kindling. She gave her a loaf of bread, instructing her to drop crumbs along the path to mark her way home.

MOTHER. What about Hansel?

ALIDA. Who?

MOTHER. Hansel and Gretel. And the woodcutter.

ALIDA. That's not how I tell the story.

MOTHER. Keep your head up, Alida.

ALIDA. *Ow! Mom!* That's not how I tell the story.

MOTHER. Well I beg your pardon. Please continue.

ALIDA. Gretel pushed into the woods, gathering kindling in her voluminous skirts, dropping breadcrumbs behind her. So intent was she that only the cawing of an evening crow drew her attention to shadows rising up the trees. She turned homeward and saw – a squirrel – and clutched in its tiny claws – a breadcrumb. The squirrel's eyes glittered, and it was gone. All the breadcrumbs were gone. Gretel found herself surrounded by an infinite, indifferent darkness.

MOTHER. *An infinite, indifferent darkness* – ? Where do you get this stuff?

ALIDA. I made it up.

MOTHER. But that phrase. You must have read it somewhere. And I thought it was birds who stole the crumbs. Not squirrels.

ALIDA. That's not how I tell the story.

MOTHER. When does she get to the witch's house?

ALIDA. That's coming. Do you want me to finish or not?

MOTHER. Okay, okay. Go ahead.

ALIDA. Gretel's fingers grew bloody from pushing hours through the roots and branches. The slithery pawsteps of ravenous creatures drew closer and closer. Just as she was about to give herself to the night, she saw – through the trees – a tiny light.

It twinkled from the windows of an odd house. The walls looked like chocolate flesh, and criss-crossing the roof were shiny white lines, like strands of mucous, glittering in the light of the moon. The front door was made of roots – or was it bones? – and lining the walkway were hairy plumes of cotton candy. Gretel knelt over one, and as it melted beneath her tongue, heard the front door *creeeeeeeak*, open, like a rusty eyelid.

(MOTHER stops brushing ALIDA's hair, troubled.)

An old woman was silhouetted in the doorway. She regarded Gretel, who found herself floating up the walkway and following the woman into her house. The front door closed behind them. The end.

MOTHER. The end?

ALIDA. The end.

MOTHER. What happens to Gretel?

(ALIDA shrugs. MOTHER stares at her in the mirror.)

Well don't tell Tom that "story." He'll be here any minute. You look adorable.

ALIDA. He's your date. Why do I have to look adorable?

MOTHER. Every little bit helps.

ALIDA. Is he going to stay over?

MOTHER. If he does, it will be like a slumber party.

(ALIDA makes a face.)

Don't make that face – it'll freeze that way. And please. Do not say anything to Tom about an infinite, indifferent darkness.

(Something changes back. Etc.)

ETYMOLOGY

(**MOTHER** *becomes* **BETH**, *taking notes longhand.*
ALIDA *dictates.*)

BETH. Tom was the Bible salesman?

ALIDA. The shoelace manufacturer.

BETH. Your mother was social.

ALIDA. That's a very nice word for it.

BETH. She was looking for love.

ALIDA. Another nice word.

BETH. Don't you believe in love? My boyfriend's a musician,
and last night he sang me this beautiful –

ALIDA. Ten a.m. Time's up.

BETH. But we just got –

ALIDA. This is all I can take of her. Or you.

BETH. Okay.

ALIDA. For tomorrow I'd like you to look up the etymology
of the word 'femur.'

BETH. The what?

ALIDA. Etymology. The derivation or history of a word. For
instance, the etymology of the word *etymology* is from
the Greek *etymon*, which means "true sense" plus *logos*,
which means "word." It is the story of a word. Another
point of reference.

BETH. Cool. I'll look it up online.

ALIDA. No, you'll look it up at the library. The old lady on
the third floor can show you how to cross reference a
variety of dictionaries and encyclopedias, some going
all the way back to when the word first *(noticing* **BETH**'s
expression) what?

BETH. It sounds time consuming.

ALIDA. This isn't community college. I don't want cliff
notes. I want information of substance.

BETH. But you – we – don't have much time. If we want to
get to the end.

ALIDA. Why do we have to get to the end?

BETH. So we get the whole story.

ALIDA. No one is going to read it.

BETH. Of course they will. This'll be *huge*.

ALIDA. No one will read it because I'm not going to publish it.

(**BETH** *blinks at her.*)

BETH. Then what's the point of writing it?

ALIDA. There is none.

BETH. You don't want to share yourself?

ALIDA. Hell no.

BETH. Then what am I doing here?

ALIDA. I keep asking myself that.

BETH. What about the other books?

ALIDA. I needed money.

BETH. You share yourself in them.

ALIDA. No, they're fiction.

BETH. But I know you now, through all of those characters.

ALIDA. *(scornful)* You know me. You don't know me.

BETH. Maybe not all of you –

ALIDA. What am I then?

BETH. You are. A woman. You are. A writer. You are. Brave.

ALIDA. Those are just words. They have nothing to do with who I am.

BETH. If words are so unimportant, why are you sending me to the library to look up the entire history of a single one?

(**ALIDA** *looks her over, grudgingly impressed.*)

ALIDA. Perhaps I'm writing it for myself.

BETH. Okay…

ALIDA. Does that work for you?

BETH. Sure…

ALIDA. That doesn't seem like it works for you.

BETH. It's just…publishing something could put the record straight.

ALIDA. There is no record. I don't allow biographies, even on the covers of my books.

BETH. You have a Wikipedia page.

ALIDA. A what?

BETH. It's an online encyclopedia. You've got a page.

ALIDA. Who put it there?

BETH. Anyone can put stuff there.

ALIDA. Anyone?

BETH. It's public domain.

ALIDA. If it's about me, it's *not* public domain. It's private domain. It's *my* domain.

BETH. The information stays up as long as everyone else agrees it's true.

ALIDA. That's terrible! How does anyone know what's true?

BETH. Is it true about your mom?

ALIDA. What about my mom?

(**ALIDA** *is suddenly like ice.*)

BETH. That she was…

ALIDA. That she was what?

BETH. That she was…

ALIDA. What?

BETH. …an arts enthusiast?

ALIDA. You know what my mom was? This is what she was!

(**ALIDA** *sweeps a drinking glass onto the floor. It shatters.*)

HIGH HEELS

(Sound of a glass splinter crash.)

MOTHER. Alida!

ALIDA. I didn't mean to!

MOTHER. I saw you do it! Now there is glass all over the floor! And Richard will be here any minute!

ALIDA. Let him clean it up.

MOTHER. He is our guest!

ALIDA. Your guest.

MOTHER. Don't you start. He's good for a man. He has a lovely singing voice.

ALIDA. He broke that bottle of gin.

MOTHER. We were dancing.

ALIDA. Why did you have to clean it up? Why did you say you were sorry?

MOTHER. He'd had a lot to drink.

ALIDA. He always has a lot to drink.

MOTHER. He's had a hard life. Richard's parents were very mean to him. When he gets angry, it really means he's sad. When he gets angry, you have to feel sorry for him. And remember the good things he does. Like sing beautiful songs on his ukulele.

ALIDA. I don't think they're beautiful.

MOTHER. Oh I do. Beautiful and sad. Like a dream.

(ALIDA looks at the floor.)

ALIDA. I'll clean the glass.

MOTHER. You'll cut your feet.

ALIDA. I'll get my shoes.

MOTHER. The soles are too thin. I have my heels. I'll clean up the glass.

(MOTHER crunches through the glass in her heels.)

ALIDA. I'll hold the dust bin.

(ALIDA kneels on the table. MOTHER sweeps up the glass and dumps it in the trash. Long moments working together. They finish.)

MOTHER. You are such a big help. See? You broke that glass to remind me how much I need you.

TEXT MESSAGES

ALIDA. Where are you going?

BETH. It's noon.

ALIDA. Noon? What are you still doing here?

BETH. I work until –

ALIDA. Ten a.m.

BETH. No, we moved it to noon.

ALIDA. We did?

BETH. To give you – us – more time.

ALIDA. It feels short.

BETH. I was at the library this morning. Two hours.

ALIDA. What were you doing there?

BETH. Looking up the word *dream.*

ALIDA. Dream. That's all you've done today. Why do you keep staring at that phone?

BETH. I'm expecting a text.

ALIDA. From whom?

BETH. My boyfriend.

ALIDA. He makes you anxious.

BETH. We had a fight. He doesn't like my stuffed animals in his apartment.

ALIDA. Get your own apartment.

BETH. I don't want to be alone.

ALIDA. Something wrong with being alone?

BETH. Not if you're good at it. I'm just not good at it. It feels like I don't exist.

ALIDA. Get a roommate. Get a dog.

BETH. It's not the same. You have your words. Your points of reference. He is my point of reference.

ALIDA. How many "texts" have you sent him?

BETH. I don't know. Ten?

ALIDA. Ten?

BETH. And he won't text me back.

ALIDA. Why should he? You're on the line.

BETH. He loves me! Why wouldn't he care that I'm anxious and sad?

ALIDA. Because you picked someone to remind you you're not worth that.

(BETH opens her mouth. Closes her mouth.)

BETH. Last night I kept dreaming I was waking up. I was waking up and looking at the clock, but as hard as I tried, I couldn't tell what time it was. I kept rolling over to hold on to my boyfriend, but he was always gone.

ALIDA. Last night I dreamt I met a family trying to cultivate human-like squirrels. There was a squirrel dressed up in a business suit. This was the most successful squirrel. He told me without speaking that his success lay in selling people the illusion of time. He told me if I wanted to see through the illusion, I would give him my clothes. I woke up naked, not knowing what time it is.

BETH. I used to wake up in a different bed every year. My father was in the military. They move people around to keep them disoriented. So their only allegiance is to what remains constant, which is the military.

ALIDA. Points of reference.

BETH. When I woke up for real, he was throwing my stuffed animals into the hall.

ALIDA. Tell him you pay half the rent.

BETH. Well.

ALIDA. You have two jobs. You can't make rent?

BETH. I lost the job at the clinic.

ALIDA. What?

BETH. I already told you.

ALIDA. When?

BETH. When did I lose the job, or when did I tell you?

ALIDA. Did they fire you?

BETH. I thought the health care field was a nurturing place. I thought there I'd be needed. But it's cold and competitive and filled with paperwork. Plus my credit cards are eating me alive. Can I work for you full time?

ALIDA. You call this work?

BETH. I got that word you wanted.

ALIDA. Which word?

BETH. Dream? The etymology? *(referring to notes)* Circa year twelve hundred fifty in the sense "sequence of sensations passing through a sleeping person's mind," probably related to the German *traum,* "deception, illusion, phantasm," Old Norse *draugr,* "ghost, apparition," or *trügen,* "to deceive, delude."

ALIDA. *(pause)* That's it?

BETH. Uh huh.

ALIDA. That's what you were doing in the library for two hours?

BETH. This morning was – hard. My stuffed animals were in the hall.

ALIDA. Did you go to the library at all?

BETH. Yes. *(pause)* No.

ALIDA. Where did you get that reference?

BETH. *(pause)* Etymonline dot com.

(**BETH** *cringes, waiting for the storm. But* **ALIDA** *goes dreadfully calm.*)

ALIDA. You thought I'd buy that?

BETH. I thought I'd make up the time tomorrow. I'm bringing sticky notes. To label the kitchen.

ALIDA. That's not what I pay you for.

BETH. The neighbors say you left something burning.

ALIDA. The neighbors are snoops and liars. You're no better.

BETH. It's not a good day.

ALIDA. Waiting for a text. To make you feel a certain way.

BETH. I just need to know he wants me.

ALIDA. You want his attention? Start running away.

BETH. What if he lets me go?

ALIDA. Then his love is a dream. And maybe without it you'll see you still exist.

FORTUNE COOKIES

(A restaurant. Sound of a woman singing a love song in Chinese.)

MOTHER. We're moving out west! Harry asked us to come.

ALIDA. When were you going to tell me?

MOTHER. I'm telling you now. You'll love it out west. There are palm trees.

ALIDA. Who's Harry?

MOTHER. Remember we met him at the Christmas party? He was contemplating a divorce. Now it's going through.

ALIDA. Are you going to marry him?

MOTHER. Eventually. He wired twenty dollars. How do you think we're able to eat out tonight? He told me to buy you some black patent leather shoes.

ALIDA. I hate patent leather shoes.

MOTHER. And they hate you. But you're not destroying these. Harry's the kind of man we deserve. I want you to look the part.

ALIDA. If we keep moving, I will never make friends.

MOTHER. Harry has kids your age.

ALIDA. Ew.

MOTHER. What?

ALIDA. I hate kids my age.

MOTHER. That's why you don't make friends.

ALIDA. Are they going to be my siblings?

MOTHER. What an awful word. I don't know where you get words like that. Yes, eventually they will be your *brother* and *sister*. In the meantime, I will be their nanny.

ALIDA. Nanny?

MOTHER. For appearances' sake. So we can live in the house. Until the divorce goes through. It's a very big house. Harry is a movie producer. Isn't that exciting?

ALIDA. I hate movies.

MOTHER. You do not.

ALIDA. They are stupid and fake.

MOTHER. They are dreams. Dreams we want to be real. But you have to go out and get them. A dream is nothing until you make it real. Now come on. Palm trees! Let's see what our fortunes say.

(*She breaks her fortune cookie in half.*)

"Careful the dream you choose to follow." Hm. What does yours say?

(**ALIDA** *breaks her fortune cookie in half.*)

ALIDA. "You will live a life without end."

MOTHER. What does that mean? These are strange fortunes. Maybe we got bad cookies. I'm going to ask for two more. Yoo hoo!

ALIDA. We don't need more cookies.

MOTHER. Maybe you don't. But I want one. Excuse me!

ALIDA. Mom!

MOTHER. I'm just calling the waitress over.

ALIDA. Why do you have to yell?

MOTHER. I am not yelling.

ALIDA. Yes you are.

MOTHER. No I'm not.

(**ALIDA** *brings her fist down on her fortune cookie halves.*)

Alida!

(**ALIDA** *brings her fist down on* **MOTHER**'*s fortune cookie halves. Pause.*)

You never liked it here. You just want to hold on to it because it's about to be gone.

STICKY NOTES

ALIDA. You're late.

BETH. The bus. It's raining.

ALIDA. You were late yesterday.

BETH. No.

ALIDA. Yes.

BETH. I don't think you're. Remembering correctly.

ALIDA. I remember fine.

BETH. I've been on time all week.

ALIDA. What day is it?

BETH. Friday.

ALIDA. When were you last late?

BETH. A couple weeks ago.

ALIDA. No. You were late today. And yesterday. You're taking advantage of my…my…

BETH. I am not taking advantage of your condition.

(**ALIDA** *writes on a sticky note.*)

ALIDA. L. I. A. R.

(*She sticks the note on* **BETH.**)

BETH. What's this?

ALIDA. That's what you are.

BETH. I am. A sticky note?

ALIDA. You are. A liar.

BETH. It was only an hour.

ALIDA. For all I know, you're late every day. Every day you lie to me. I take you on full time, and this is how you repay me.

BETH. Alida, at this point paranoia is natural.

ALIDA. Don't tell me what's natural! Where's my story?

BETH. It's right here.

ALIDA. You took it home with you! I couldn't find it!

BETH. It hasn't left the apartment.

ALIDA. Where's my word?

BETH. *Witch?*

ALIDA. The word I assigned you.

BETH. Yeah, the word *witch*. Old English *wicce*, "female magician, sorceress," Lower German "soothsayer, healer," Proto Germanic *wikkjaz*, which means "neuromancer," or one who wakes the dead, and in Anglo-Saxon glossaries, *wicce* also stands for *divinatricem*, derived from the Latin *divinus*: noun, "southsayer," verb, "to make out by supernatural insight," adjective, "of god," and Proto-Indo-European *divinawickjim*, meaning wisdom beyond words, the other which is also the self.

ALIDA. *Diviniwickjim?* Did you make that up?

BETH. No! That's what the lady said.

ALIDA. What lady?

BETH. The old lady at the library. The one you told me to –

ALIDA. You're making all kinds of stuff up. You think you can get anything by me now.

BETH. We should look into adjusting your meds.

ALIDA. Drugging me up so you can steal my story. Because you are a…a…

   (She squints at **BETH***'s sticky note.)*

   …liar!

BETH. I am not a –

ALIDA. You said you were late today because of the bus. That is not true. You were late today because you were – yakking – on your *(She holds her hand to her ear.)*. I was up here in the window watching you. You yakked for an hour straight, then you came up here and told me it was the rain.

BETH. That's a. Small lie.

ALIDA. Who were you yakking to?

BETH. My boyfriend.

ALIDA. I might have known. You were crying. And waving your hand. Like it might make you better...make you better... *(waving her hand)* ...

BETH. Understood?

ALIDA. I will no longer be needing your services.

BETH. I don't think you know what that means.

ALIDA. It means you won't be able to trick me anymore. I don't need you to finish my story. I can do it on my own. I am a... I am a...what? WHAT AM I GODDAM IT??

(She flings her pad of sticky notes at **BETH***.* **BETH** *doesn't flinch as they hit her in the chest.* **BETH** *picks up the pad and writes:)*

BETH. W. R. I. T. E. R. You are a writer.

(She sticks the note on **ALIDA***.)*

Can I take this off?

(She peels off her own note and lets it drift to the floor. **ALIDA** *looks her up and down.)*

ALIDA. You are still a liar.

BONES

(Sound of the wind on the desert.)

MOTHER. Here it is. Harry's house.

ALIDA. Palm trees.

MOTHER. They were brought here from Egypt. That's what Harry said. I love it here already.

ALIDA. That's what Harry said.

MOTHER. He produces movies. Look at those white columns. We have a whole suite of rooms to ourselves.

ALIDA. The servant's quarters.

MOTHER. It's temporary. Soon we'll move downstairs.

ALIDA. The columns look like bones. With knobs at the top and bottom. Like femurs.

MOTHER. Where do you get words like that?

ALIDA. From the Latin "*thighbone.*" Also *femial,* an architectural term meaning "that which holds up what will some day fall down."

MOTHER. You are too smart to be my daughter.

ALIDA. Do you wish I were stupid?

MOTHER. Of course not. It would just be easier on you if you could look at a palm tree and be happy.

ALIDA. Are you happy?

MOTHER. I will be. Once the divorce goes through.

(They peer up at the house.)

ALIDA. I'm scared.

MOTHER. Shhhh. It's a new adventure. Let's go in.

TEARS I

(ALIDA's apartment. Nighttime. BETH is at the window. Beside her is a big, black garbage bag. ALIDA stands in her robe.)

ALIDA. What are you doing here? It's the middle of the night.

BETH. I don't know where else to go.

ALIDA. How did you get in?

BETH. You gave me a key.

ALIDA. I did?

BETH. Two weeks ago. When you locked yourself downstairs.

ALIDA. I'm sure it was not an invitation to –

BETH. I'm sorry. I just need a place to crash.

ALIDA. Are you – are you crying?

BETH. Yes.

ALIDA. What are you crying about?

BETH. My boyfriend is still texting his ex-girlfriend. I looked at his phone. I read all the messages. And here I've been thinking I knew him. Thinking we were growing together. Thinking I could finally trust someone. He wrote a song for me and I thought it meant he loved me. I trashed his entire music collection. I threw his computer out the window and dragged a kitchen knife across his vinyl. I can't go back.

ALIDA. You can't stay here.

BETH. Please.

TEARS II

(The servant's quarters. **MOTHER** *is at the window.)*

ALIDA. What are you doing here?

MOTHER. I was tired of the party.

ALIDA. Are you crying?

MOTHER. No.

ALIDA. You look beautiful. In that dress.

MOTHER. Thank you.

ALIDA. Does Harry like it?

MOTHER. He has guests.

ALIDA. Aren't you a guest?

MOTHER. Not yet. *(pause)* What are these leaves? On the sill?

ALIDA. I'm collecting the yellow ones. On my way home from school.

MOTHER. How is school? Are you making friends?

ALIDA. No.

MOTHER. Why not, my dear?

*(**ALIDA** shrugs.)*

What about Harry Jr. and Harriet?

ALIDA. They're horrific.

MOTHER. I want you to be a child. I want you to be happy.

ALIDA. The leaves make me happy. I love the Fall.

MOTHER. I love the Fall, too. It makes me sad.

ALIDA. Is that why you love Harry? Because he makes you sad?

MOTHER. *(pause)* Sometimes it's hard to know why you love someone.

ALIDA. Is he afraid to have you at the party?

MOTHER. He's afraid of what people will think.

ALIDA. Won't they think you are beautiful?

MOTHER. I wish people thought that way.

ALIDA. Well I think you're beautiful.

MOTHER. Oh. If I were a good mother, that would be enough.

TEARS III

ALIDA. Shut that window. It's cold in here.

BETH. The moon is out. The moon understands my suffering.

ALIDA. Why do you waste your energy on someone who doesn't love you?

BETH. He does love me.

ALIDA. Not in a way that makes you happy.

BETH. It's not all about being happy.

ALIDA. Surely some of it is.

BETH. Don't say it like that.

ALIDA. No.

BETH. Oh.

ALIDA. Don't feel sorry for me.

BETH. No.

ALIDA. I've never found it. Necessary.

BETH. But are you. Happy?

(**ALIDA** *shrugs.*)

BETH. My parents kicked me out of the house at fifteen for sleeping with an Asian boy. What was I supposed to do? – we were stationed in Korea. My therapist says I'm trying to recreate that abandonment by choosing guys who are emotionally unavailable. I keep creating the same story, becuase it's familiar, even though it keeps destroying me. She said if I see it's just a story, and has nothing to do with who I really am, I can let it go.

ALIDA. *(snorts)* Therapy.

BETH. It's been helpful.

ALIDA. Still using someone else to see yourself.

BETH. Well how else do you do it?

TEARS IV

ALIDA. You *are* crying.

MOTHER. Mothers cry, too.

ALIDA. Is Harry making you cry?

MOTHER. He's not making me. It's the way I feel when I think of him.

ALIDA. Are you in love?

(**MOTHER** *is mildly surprised she knows what this is.*)

MOTHER. Yes.

ALIDA. I thought that was good.

MOTHER. It's good. And it's bad. It's wonderful. And it hurts.

ALIDA. Why does it hurt?

MOTHER. Maybe because, when you're in it, you're afraid it will go away.

ALIDA. I will never be in love.

MOTHER. Why not?

ALIDA. Because it makes you sad.

MOTHER. Sometimes that's what happens when you open yourself to other people.

ALIDA. I only want to be with you.

MOTHER. I won't always be around. You have to be with other people.

ALIDA. How come?

MOTHER. Because they show who you are.

ALIDA. Does Harry show you who you are?

MOTHER. In some ways, he does. In some ways, we are alike.

(*pause*)

ALIDA. We could leave.

MOTHER. Where would we go?

ALIDA. North. We could live in a house of snow. And drink from glasses made of ice. And drive a pack of huskies. And sleep with them at night.

MOTHER. I thought you were tired of moving.

ALIDA. I want you to be happy.

    (MOTHER takes ALIDA's hand.)

MOTHER. Right now, I am.

TEARS V

(**ALIDA** *pulls away from* **BETH**.)

ALIDA. So this is this how you do it.

BETH. What?

ALIDA. Worm your way in.

BETH. I'm not – I don't know where else –

ALIDA. You need to find your own place.

BETH. *(entreating)* I'm looking. I'm looking for my own place.

(**ALIDA** *sighs. Deep and grumpy.*)

ALIDA. Three nights. That's all I can bear.

STUFFED ANIMALS

(Daytime. **ALIDA** *stares down at the garbage bag.)*

ALIDA. What's this?

BETH. *(holding up a pill box)* M is for Monday. T is for Tuesday. W is Wednesday. TH is Thursday. F is Friday. S is Saturday. SU is Sunday. You've been confusing your medications. You need to take the pills in the compartment that marks the day.

ALIDA. No this. *(indicating the garbage bag)*

BETH. Those are my stuffed animals.

ALIDA. What are they doing here –

BETH. You said I could stay.

ALIDA. But only for…what's today?

BETH. Today is Tuesday. So we'll start with T.

ALIDA. How many days have you been here?

BETH. Two days.

ALIDA. You're only supposed to be here for…

BETH. Three.

ALIDA. So you leave tomorrow.

BETH. Yes.

ALIDA. Good. Where are you going?

BETH. Back to my night job. I need money.

ALIDA. I pay you.

BETH. You haven't paid me in over a month.

ALIDA. I paid you just last week.

BETH. That was last month.

ALIDA. What about the clinic?

BETH. I quit a long time ago. I didn't like they way they were treating me. I'm tired of being taken for granted. I went back to my night job.

ALIDA. Where is my story?

BETH. It's right here.

ALIDA. You took it last night.

BETH. You've been hiding it from me.

ALIDA. Because you've been taking it from me.

BETH. I spend half an hour each day looking for it. We don't have time to –

ALIDA. This is about none of the material leaving my apartment!

BETH. Okay! Here's the number if you need me. On this sticky by the phone. I had to cancel my cell.

ALIDA. Where is this?

BETH. A nightclub. I serve cocktails.

ALIDA. Don't come home stinking of gin.

(**BETH** *giggles*.)

ALIDA. You think that's funny? Tomorrow you go. Today is. What's today?

BETH. Tuesday.

ALIDA. Tuesday is…

BETH. T.

ALIDA. Today is T. Tomorrow is W. You get the hell out of here on W.

BETH. You've had your meds today. See, T is empty?

ALIDA. You're leaving?

BETH. I have to go to work. I'm leaving my number on this sticky by the phone.

BASEMENTS

ALIDA. Where are you going?

MOTHER. Downstairs. Like I do every night.

ALIDA. Where do you go?

MOTHER. To visit with Harry.

ALIDA. All night long?

MOTHER. Sometimes we stay up so late it becomes early.

ALIDA. What do you with him?

MOTHER. I help him make dreams.

ALIDA. Good dreams or bad dreams?

    (**MOTHER** *looks at her sharply.*)

MOTHER. What was it that woke you up?

ALIDA. A bad dream.

MOTHER. About what?

ALIDA. About Harry's movie.

MOTHER. Harry's made lots of movies.

ALIDA. About the one he's making in the basement.

MOTHER. How do you know about the basement?

ALIDA. He told me.

MOTHER. What did he –

ALIDA. Not to go in.

MOTHER. That's right. You shouldn't go in.

ALIDA. Have you ever gone in?

MOTHER. *(pause)* No.

ALIDA. So you don't know what's in the basement?

MOTHER. *(pause)* No.

ALIDA. So you wouldn't know if my dream is true.

MOTHER. What did you dream?

ALIDA. That Harry was holding someone down. And making her cry.

MOTHER. Harry. Would not do that.

ALIDA. He did not want to be doing it. But he could not help himself.

MOTHER. What do you mean?

ALIDA. He creates all these beautiful dreams, but he knows they'll never be real. This makes him sad. And sometimes cruel. So he has to make bad dreams, because these are closer to his experience.

(Pause.)

MOTHER. I'm sorry you had a bad dream. You know it isn't real.

ALIDA. When I woke up, you were gone.

MOTHER. I was downstairs. And guess what?

ALIDA. What?

MOTHER. Harry's divorce is going through. You can move downstairs, too.

ALIDA. To the basement?

MOTHER. No. No. To a beautiful room of your own.

PEEP SHOWS

BETH. You did go down.

ALIDA. I don't remember.

BETH. What was down there?

ALIDA. What are you writing?

BETH. You're writing. Your story.

ALIDA. I'm not writing. You are.

BETH. I'm writing down what you say.

ALIDA. So you can sell it?

BETH. No.

ALIDA. It would make a lot of money.

BETH. Do you want it published?

ALIDA. Otherwise what's the point?

    (**BETH** *gives her a long look.*)

BETH. Do you have a will?

ALIDA. Who would I leave anything to?

BETH. Or a lawyer?

ALIDA. I hate lawyers.

BETH. We should have done this sooner.

ALIDA. We're not finished yet.

BETH. I think we need to hurry. We need to get to the end.

ALIDA. There is no end.

BETH. What was happening in the basement?

ALIDA. I don't remember.

BETH. See, I think you do. I think you're hiding.

ALIDA. Don't examine me. That's not what I pay you for.

BETH. You haven't paid me yet.

ALIDA. You have to remind me to get out my checkbook.

BETH. I just thought. Since you're letting me stay here.

ALIDA. But only for. Three nights. Right? What day is it?

BETH. Tuesday.

ALIDA. No, what day on here? *(indicating the pill box)*

BETH. T.

ALIDA. What day are you supposed to leave?

BETH. W.

ALIDA. So you've been here two nights.

BETH. *(pause)* Right. But. I like it here.

ALIDA. You can't stay.

BETH. Why not?

ALIDA. Nobody stays.

BETH. I will stay.

ALIDA. You leave at night.

BETH. I have another job.

ALIDA. With Harry.

BETH. At the cocktail bar.

ALIDA. I found this box of matches. It says "The Voyeur." There's this woman. Behind glass.

BETH. It's a bar. And a peep show.

ALIDA. You work in the bar? Or the peep show?

BETH. I work in the bar. I used to work in the peep show.

ALIDA. Was this you behind the glass?

BETH. It used to be. Years ago. The men came in. They had a dream of a woman who wanted them. And I wanted them to want me. I thought we could make each other happy. But I always left feeling sad. When your dream is about being wanted, instead of about who you are, it's always a little sad.

ALIDA. He was making smokers. In the basement.

BETH. Smokers.

ALIDA. That was the word for them then. The men would watch them and smoke.

BETH. Is it true – that your mom –?

ALIDA. Whatever she did was never released. I took care of that.

BETH. What did you do?

ALIDA. All the smokers. Went up in smoke.

CASTLES

(Sound of a car. **MOTHER** *drives,* **ALIDA** *cringing in the passenger seat.)*

MOTHER. Alida!

ALIDA. I didn't mean to!

MOTHER. You set Harry's house on fire!

ALIDA. It was supposed to be the basement.

MOTHER. What were you thinking?

ALIDA. I didn't like it down there!

MOTHER. And the divorce was going through! We were so close!

ALIDA. Close to what?

MOTHER. We were almost! Out of the woods! I was almost! Out of the woods!

ALIDA. What woods?

MOTHER. You're not happy anywhere! I have tried and tried to find us a home!

ALIDA. You're going too fast!

(They swerve. Sound of horns. They continue on.)

Does Harry know we borrowed his car?

MOTHER. *(grim)* I'm sure he'll figure it out.

ALIDA. Where are we going?

MOTHER. South.

ALIDA. What's south?

MOTHER. Another country.

ALIDA. Can we stay there?

MOTHER. I don't know. I have to think.

ALIDA. I'm hungry.

MOTHER. We don't have any money.

ALIDA. Money?

MOTHER. Yes, money, Alida, *money!*

ALIDA. We could find some people and I could ask them for money.

MOTHER. Oh god.

ALIDA. I'm sorry.

MOTHER. It's not your fault. He didn't love me. He never loved me. I keep dragging you along. I'm a terrible mother.

ALIDA. No you're not.

MOTHER. Yes I am. I don't know what to do.

(Together they spot something in the distance.)

ALIDA. Mom! Look! A castle!

GOODBYES I

BETH. Where is it?

ALIDA. What?

BETH. The story.

ALIDA. You're the one who's supposed to remember.

BETH. It smells in here. Did you leave the oven on again?

ALIDA. I don't know what you're talking about.

BETH. The story.

ALIDA. You took it.

BETH. No I didn't.

ALIDA. I saw you sneak it out.

BETH. I brought it back.

ALIDA. I knew it! I knew you took it.

BETH. What about the castle?

ALIDA. What castle?

BETH. The castle at the end.

ALIDA. There is no end.

BETH. Of the story.

ALIDA. You took my story.

BETH. You want it published.

ALIDA. NO!

BETH. You said you –

ALIDA. I don't want to –

BETH. So people will know you.

ALIDA. I don't want to be – known –

BETH. Yes you do! Why else do you write?

ALIDA. For no one but myself.

BETH. I found your fan mail. In your closet. You've been saving it for years.

ALIDA. Liar! Snoop! Succubus!

BETH. You needed a clean pair of underwear.

ALIDA. Leaves! Mucous! Squirrels!

BETH. I didn't get back until morning. You were frantic.

ALIDA. Frantic?

BETH. You kept saying I was supposed to be back before you wake up.

ALIDA. I don't remember.

BETH. I found you on the street.

ALIDA. I was on the street?

BETH. You said you were looking for the library.

ALIDA. Points of reference.

BETH. I caught you downstairs, in the boiler room.

ALIDA. Down in the basement.

BETH. Harry was making porn.

ALIDA. Agh! I hate that word.

BETH. Porn! Porn! Porn! It's just a word, right? It doesn't mean anything, right?

ALIDA. I'm sick. Why are you doing this to me?

BETH. I think if you told the story, you could let it go.

ALIDA. I already did.

BETH. What?

ALIDA. Let it go.

(ALIDA *produces the now-thick manila folder, filled with note pads. Everything is burnt to a crisp.*)

BETH. Oh my god.

ALIDA. Ah hah.

BETH. You could have set the whole place on fire.

ALIDA. You wanted to sell it.

BETH. I wanted –

ALIDA. – to put yourself in it. To put a page up online. And tell everyone you saved me.

BETH. You saved me. You gave me a home.

ALIDA. You weren't here for me. You just wanted the story.

BETH. I already knew the story. I wanted to know how you would tell it.

(ALIDA *falters. Then draws herself upright.*)

ALIDA. What day was yesterday?

BETH. Tuesday.

ALIDA. No. On here.

BETH. T.

ALIDA. So today is –

BETH. W.

ALIDA. You're supposed to leave on W. Right?

BETH. *(pause)* Right.

ALIDA. You were supposed to leave. Many W's ago. But you've been. *Lying.* Telling me it's only been. Two nights. It's always supposed to be. Tomorrow. But I've been making marks. See here on this sticky? It hasn't been. Two nights. It's been. *Weeks.*

BETH. You don't remember. You're the one who won't let me leave.

ALIDA. You keep telling me it's been two nights.

BETH. You keep telling *me* it's been two nights.

ALIDA. No. You keep telling me it's T. And that you will leave on W.

BETH. No. You keep telling *me* it's T. And that I can't leave until W.

ALIDA. I don't. Believe you.

BETH. Clearly.

ALIDA. I don't. Trust you.

BETH. You don't trust anyone.

ALIDA. You need to leave. Right now.

BETH. I don't think that's a good idea.

ALIDA. Peep show! Weakling! WHORE!

(This hits **BETH** *hard.)*

BETH. Okay.

ALIDA. And I'm going to pay you.

BETH. That isn't necessary. You've put me up.

ALIDA. Where is my check book?

BETH. That isn't necessary.

ALIDA. WHERE IS MY –

BETH. Here! It's right here.

ALIDA. How much to I owe you? How many hours have you worked for me? I'm going to have to depend on you to remember. Here is your chance to take me to…take me to…the washing place.

BETH. The cleaners?

ALIDA. As long as I owe you nothing.

(*Pause.*)

BETH. I have given you a lot of room because of your illness. And because I realized how much we are alike. But I'm done forcing myself on people. If you want me to stay, you're going to have to say, I need you.

ALIDA. Never. Will I ever say that.

BETH. Then try this word: Goodbye.

GOODBYES II

(At the gates of Disneyland.)

ALIDA. What's this?

MOTHER. Your ticket.

ALIDA. This isn't what I thought.

MOTHER. I kept asking Harry to take us to Disneyland, but he never would.

ALIDA. I thought it was a real castle.

MOTHER. It's Sleeping Beauty's Castle.

ALIDA. Sleeping Beauty gives me the creeps.

MOTHER. Come on! Be a kid! Here's some money. Go buy yourself a corn fritter. Or a horse and carriage ride. Or cotton candy.

ALIDA. I thought we didn't have any –

MOTHER. *(gesturing off)* That nice man paid for it. There are a lot of nice people here. Families.

ALIDA. Fat families.

MOTHER. Alida!

ALIDA. What?

MOTHER. Can't I do anything to make you happy?

(ALIDA trembles.)

ALIDA. I want. To be happy. I'm trying. To be happy.

MOTHER. You shouldn't have to try.

ALIDA. If you like it here, I do, too. Cotton candy sounds good. Let's go in.

MOTHER. I'm not going.

ALIDA. What?

MOTHER. He paid for one ticket.

ALIDA. But –

MOTHER. It's okay. I'll wait here for you.

ALIDA. I don't want to go without you.

MOTHER. You won't have me all your life. You have to learn to do things alone.

ALIDA. Right now??

(**MOTHER** *pauses, wraps her arms around* **ALIDA.**)

MOTHER. No matter where you are, I will always be with
you.

ALIDA. Are you crying?

MOTHER. No.

(**MOTHER** *gently extracts herself from* **ALIDA**'s *embrace.*)

MOTHER. Goodbye.

(**SHE** *disappears.* **ALIDA** *enters the park, clutching her
ticket.*)

THE WITCH

(The wind picks up and the trees press in.)

ALIDA. The little girl crept along the path, dropping crumbs of cotton candy, telling herself stories to keep the fear at bay. Stories of other lost girls, fairy tales with beautiful words and sensible meanings and obvious ends. But as darkness fell, she began to suspect, as in some ways she'd always suspected, they were nothing but lies. Lies to keep her from the truth, the truth of the Universe, the truth of now – a dark and wild nothing!

*(**ALIDA** looks around, ill at ease.)*

She tries to see her hand before her.

*(**ALIDA** looks at her hand.)*

It is that of an old woman! She peers back along the forest path –

*(**ALIDA** turns back.)*

The crumbs – the words – are gone!

*(**ALIDA** is terrified. Then. In the clearing, a house becomes visible. The door opens with an agonizing creak. The Witch stand silhouetted in the doorway.)*

*(She and **ALIDA** regard each other. The Witch looks at the phone. **ALIDA** shuffles to it, picks up the receiver. Carefully, painstakingly, dials the number on the sticky note. The Witch removes her mask. Underneath is **BETH**. **ALIDA**'s lips move, but she cannot form any words.)*

BETH. Alida?

LEAVES

(BETH brushes ALIDA's hair. Several strokes in silence.)

BETH. It's Fall again.

ALIDA. It's Fall.

BETH. Did you see the leaves on the window sill?

(ALIDA turns to look.)

We should take a walk later. In the park.

ALIDA. Okay.

(Several more strokes. The brush catches. ALIDA whimpers, childlike.)

Ow!

BETH. Sorry. Your hair is so fine.

ALIDA. Hurts! Hurts.

BETH. I'll go more slowly. Okay?

ALIDA. Okay.

(Several more strokes. Slower.)

ALIDA. Mother?

BETH. I'm Beth.

ALIDA. Beth?

BETH. Yes. I take care of you.

ALIDA. I remember.

BETH. You remember I take care of you?

ALIDA. No. Mother.

BETH. You remember your mother?

ALIDA. Yes. You are.

BETH. Beth. I am Beth.

ALIDA. I am.

BETH. You are. Alida.

ALIDA. I am.

BETH. You are. Alida.

ALIDA. I am.

BETH. You are. A writer. See?

*(She points to the writer sticky note on **ALIDA**.)*

ALIDA. A writer.

(She looks to the window sill.)

A leaf.

BETH. Yes, those are leaves. *(pause)* We should walk later. In the park.

WOODS

(**ALIDA** *shuffles on* **BETH***'s arm. She takes tiny, careful steps. Their progress is extremely slow. Sound of the strong wind through the trees in Fall. Sticky notes float down from the sky.*)

BETH. I love the Fall. It makes me feel I am happy and sad at the same time. Which is a great feeling. Like being everything you are all at once. All those things you thought were so important, all the words you used to tell the stories about who you are...are nothing. Because once you know the story, you do not need the words. Once you know the person, you do not need the story. So the space between us disappears. And I am hopeful in a sad way. Or sad in a hopeful way. That's how Fall makes me feel.

(**ALIDA** *looks up at the falling sticky notes. She looks down at the 'writer' note on her chest. She pulls it off. Lets it drift down from her fingers.* **BETH** *continues to stroll.*)

Words. Window sills. Yellow leaves.

(**ALIDA** *looks ahead. In the clearing, a house becomes visible.*)

High heels. Etymology. Sticky Notes.

(**ALIDA** *moves toward the house. The front door opens.*)

Text Messages. Stuffed Animals. Fortune cookies. Bones.

(**ALIDA** *steps inside the house, silhouetted against the light.*)

Peep shows. Castles. Boyfriends. Goodbyes.

(*The front door begins to close.*)

Making lists. Reading maps. Driving far. Pulling over. To watch the trees.

(BETH stops, peers over her shoulder toward ALIDA. *The front door closes.)*

Learning. Like the leaves. To let you go.

THE END